Misty Morgan

Written by: Stephen Cosgrove
Illustrated by: Robin James

A Serendipity™ Book

PRICE STERN SLOAN, INC.

D0006558

SECOND PRINTING — AUGUST 1987

Copyright © 1987 by Price Stern Sloan, Inc.
Published by Price Stern Sloan, Inc.
360 North La Cienega Boulevard, Los Angeles, California 90048

ISBN 0-8431-1910-1

Dedicated to the memory of my brother Robert, who died without seeing what I have seen, but shared so much that I might see what I have seen.

Stephen

If you gazed beyond the crashing waves and rolling tides to the place where the sea becomes sky, you would find an emerald island where rainbows begin and the moon rests after each night's journey.

It was from this island that dreams came forth and spread themselves like a gentle fog across the land, bringing children bits of delight when they closed their eyes and went to sleep... dreams of a gentler time and place.

Now on this island of dreams was a castle, a magnificent thing of heavy stone, draped in ivy with a worn, wooden drawbridge that was always left down. Hanging from every wall were clocks that ticked and tocked the whole day through. There were alarm clocks, cuckoo clocks, grandfather clocks, and even a grandmother clock that hung beside the stove in the kitchen.

It was in this castle that a princess lived, a very pretty princess dressed in pinks and purples. The very pretty princess lived by time and time alone. She would rush from one clock to the other, always checking the time. She was always rushing here and rushing there, crying, "Can't be late!" Everything here was on a schedule and time was the master and the princess was the slave.

Now, the princess didn't live alone on the island, for she had a friend, who was a wonderful unicorn by the name of "Morgan." He had a coat of silver hair and his tail and mane were woven of silk and satin. He wore upon his head a horn that was twisted like golden taffy.

Morgan loved to play and frolic in the forest and meadows of the emerald isle. He would munch a bunch of clover here and sip some dew from the honeysuckle vine over there. He would chase after butterflies and kick at the sun, for his life was his own and filled with fun.

One day, Morgan went to the castle to play. His hooves thundered and rumbled as he walked across the drawbridge, looking for his friend the princess. He clicked his way down the cobblestone hallways, peeking in here and snuffling in there.

Suddenly, the princess dashed by, running hither and thither on her carefully scheduled rounds. Morgan tossed his mane and stomped his foot, anxious to play, but she rushed on.

"I don't have time to play right now, silly unicorn," she said as she looked at her watch. "Maybe later...maybe later." With that she was gone in a flurry of skirts.

Morgan didn't mind. He had plenty of time, so he went back outside to wait. He watched the sun slip from morning to noon and then, sure that he had waited long enough, meandered back to the castle of time.

Once again, he clicked and clunked his way back inside to play with the princess. He found her winding a clock that had lost its tock. Again, he tossed his mane and stomped his foot, eager to play.

"Silly, silly unicorn!" she said impatiently, as she yanked on the cord of a cuckoo clock. "I don't have time to play right now! Come back later!" And she was off again, doing those things that needed to be done right now.

He waited and waited. A day, maybe two, passed by while he nibbled on some flowers and chased a bird about the meadow. He idly spent his time scratching his back on the bark of a tree, or taking naps in the bright, golden sunlight. He waited, and whiled away the time. Finally, he hurried back to the castle.

Morgan tossed his mane excitedly as he pranced into the castle and down the massive hallways. With sputtering candles throwing dancing light about him, he wandered from room to room, but nowhere could he find the princess.

In desperation, he looked in the basement coal room, and there he found the princess shoveling coal into a bucket. He reared, tossing his hooves eagerly into the air, and whinnied just once, ready to play.

The princess looked up, and with the back of her hand pushed an errant curl out of the way, leaving a coal smudge in its place. "Listen, unicorn!" she said impatiently, "I am very, very busy. Time is wasting and I don't have time to play right now. When I do have time to play I'll find you! For now, *leave me be!*" With that, she grabbed the coal bucket, and in a puff of black dust, zipped up the stairs.

Morgan slowly dropped his head and, with heavy hooves, left the castle keep.

Morgan was very upset by what the princess had said. He had waited and waited, but she had never wanted to play. He wandered far away from the princess and the castle of time.

He walked aimlessly until he came to a mystical place called "The Misty Meadows." Here, the fog slipped and sneaked about the forests, making everything seem invisible. A lonely place, so quiet and empty that even the birds wouldn't sing.

Morgan was so upset by what the princess had said that he didn't really know where he was going. Before you could say, "unicorn" twice, he had walked into the Misty Meadows and disappeared from sight.

The princess stayed in the castle, winding the clocks one by one until they were all wound. She did the chores—from sweeping halls to shaking rugs. She worked by the clock until, one day, she noticed that Morgan hadn't been around in some time. "Hmm," she thought, "I wonder where that pesky unicorn has gone?"

She took off her apron, and went outside to look. She looked around the castle walls, but he wasn't there. She looked in the orchard and down by the pond, but nowhere could he be found.

Frightened now because she couldn't find him, she began to follow his hoof prints down the path and away from the castle.

The princess walked and walked, until she came to the fog that shrouded the Misty Meadows. "Oh, no!" she cried. "He couldn't have gone in there! No one or no thing has ever gone into the Misty Meadows and ever come out!"

She paced about at the edge of the meadow, but she could only find traces of Morgan going in, never coming out.

"I've got to find him!" the princess cried. She ran about the forest, gathering a great arm-load of pine cones. Then, she began to follow Morgan's hoof prints in the Misty Meadows. Step-by-step, she carefully followed the trail, dropping a pine cone with every step so she could find her way out again. The mists swirled about her, trying to get her to lose her way, but still she pressed on, following the trail.

Finally, she reached the point where she had no more pine cones left and she could go no farther. Loudly, she shouted, "Morgan! Morgan! Come to me. It's time to play!" But all that was shouted was quickly swallowed by the fog, and she was left shrouded in silence.

Sadly, she followed the trail of pine cones back out of the Misty Meadows and into the bright light of day.

Alone, without her friend the unicorn, the saddened princess sat on a rock at the edge of the Stream of Regrets and began to cry and cry. She cried for her selfishness. She cried for those times that she didn't have time to share. And, most of all, she cried because she knew she would never see her friend Morgan again.

She sat on the rock, large tears streaming down her face, and stared into the swirling mists of the Misty Meadows. She watched and watched. She blinked back the tears and looked very hard...there! There was a shadow. Suddenly, the mists parted and there stood Morgan, bathed in the golden light of the morning sun.

The princess rushed to the unicorn and threw her arms around him. Morgan tossed his head and whinnied impatiently, eager to play the games he had waited so long to play. He knelt down, and the princess leaped on his back. Off they ran, the wind whipping at their hair.

The very last thing the princess did before they ran out of sight was to take off her watch and toss it far into the Misty Meadows, for she would never be a slave to time again.

THERE IS A TIME FOR WORK
AND A TIME FOR PLAY.
SHARE TIME WITH YOUR FRIENDS
BEFORE THEY GO AWAY!

Serendipity™ Books

Written by Stephen Cosgrove
Illustrated by Robin James

Enjoy all the delightful books in the Serendipity Series:

($1.95 each)

*also available with cassette ($4.95)

The above titles, and many others, can be bought wherever books are sold, or may be ordered directly from the publisher by sending check or money order for the amount listed, plus $1.00 for handling and mailing to Price Stern Sloan's Direct Mail Sales Division at the address below.

PRICE STERN SLOAN, INC.

360 North La Cienega Boulevard, Los Angeles, California 90048

Prices slightly higher in Canada